YO-BLW-910

This book belongs to:

_____

Jump Right In

A *Faith 'n Stuff* Book

MARY LOU CARNEY

Fleming H. Revell Company
Tarrytown, New York

This Fleming H. Revell edition published by special arrangement with Guideposts Associates, Inc.

Copyright © 1989, 1991 by Guideposts Associates, Inc., Carmel, NY 10512. All rights reserved.

No part of this book may be reproduced, stored in a retrieval system or transmitted in any form or by any means, electronic, mechanical, photocopying, recording or otherwise except for brief quotations in reviews without the written permission of the publisher. Inquiries should be addressed to the Rights and Permissions Department, Guideposts Associates, Inc., 757 Third Avenue, New York, NY 10017.

Every attempt has been made to credit the sources of copyrighted material in this book. If any such acknowledgment has been inadvertently omitted or miscredited, receipt of such information would be appreciated.

Acknowledgments

All scripture quotations, unless otherwise noted, are from the King James Version of the Bible.

Scripture verses marked (TLB) are taken from The Living Bible, copyright © 1971 owned by transfer to Illinois Marine Bank, N.A. (as trustees). Used by permission of Tyndale House Publishers, Wheaton, IL 60188.

Scripture verses marked (NIV) are from the Holy Bible, New International Version. Copyright © 1973, 1978, 1984, by International Bible Society. Used by permission of Zondervan Bible Publishers.

The cartoon on page 113 is reprinted from *Youth Specialities Clip Art Book Two*, copyright 1987 by Youth Specialties, Inc., 1224 Greenfield Dr., El Cajon, CA 92021. Used by permission.

The cartoons appearing on pages 33 and 103 are by Ron Wheeler, from his book, *Cartoon Clip Art for Youth Leaders* (Baker Book House). Used by permission.

The cartoons appearing on pages 62 and 87 are reprinted from *Outrageous Clip Art for Youth Ministry*, copyright 1988, illustrated by Rand Kruback. Published by Group Books, Box 481, Loveland, CO 80539.

Designed by Holly Johnson.
Drawings on pages 18, 22, 23, 25, 30, 31, 37, 69, 85, 95, 96, and 122 by Holly Johnson.
"Snappy Talks" and miscellaneous cartoons drawn by Stephen DeStefano.
Puzzles created by LMD Service for Publishers.

Printed in the United States of America.
ISBN 0-8007-5404-2

WHAT'S INSIDE?

Read Me First 7
October—My Calendar Page 10
   Week 1: Tons of Talent 12
   Week 2: All Fired Up 19
   Week 3: Word Power 27
   Snappy Talk 35
   Week 4: A Time to Believe in Yourself 36
   Week 5: Of Tricks and Treats 44
   Building a Better Me 53
November—My Calendar Page 54
   Week 6: Fall In! 56
   Week 7: I'll Vote for That! 64
   Snappy Talk 71
   Week 8: Pigeons and Pilgrims 72
   Week 9: I Think I Can…I Think I Can 81
   Building a Better Me 89
December—My Calendar Page 90
   Week 10: Wings and Things 92
   Week 11: Not to Be Taken Lightly 99
   Snappy Talk 107
   Week 12: My Very Best 108
   Week 13: Some New Year's Fun 116
   Building a Better Me 124
Answer Page 125

READ ME FIRST

Jump Right In. It's that time of year—time to let the air out of your inner tube, pack away your sand shovels, and trade your swimsuit for jeans and a sweatshirt. It's time to jump right in to all fall has to offer. Back-to-school friends, football games, cool Saturdays—and some super special holidays! It's time to see the Creator at work—in nature *and* in your life.

It's time to jump in to your new *Faith 'n Stuff* book, too. It's better than ever, filled with great stories about kids just like you. They have to do history projects and write stories for English. (Could you use a *magic* pencil?) They worry about school gift exchanges and make New Year's resolutions. Then there's Serendipity, a talking Christmas candle. And Sarah, whose father owns the inn—the *full* inn—in Bethlehem. Visit Guerktown and find out why Baby is the most famous of all the Guerks. Spend the afternoon with Anton and his "beasties." It all adds up to more fun than ever!

Need some help memorizing Bible verses? Having trouble wrapping your Christmas presents? No idea how to begin those thank-you notes? Check out the "Building a Better Me" pages.

Wally, our turtle friend, of course, is back. He's been waiting for you, with lots of laughs and "Snappy Talk" to share.

So, are you ready? Then let's *Jump Right In* to fun and facts and faith and stuff!

—Mary Lou Carney

Jump Right In

OCTOBER

Pumpkins round,
Spooky sounds,

Frost on the ground,
Leaves tumbling down—

October's come to town!

Burning leaves, pumpkin pies, jack-o'-lanterns, bobbing apples, hayrides, hot cocoa, and football. There's lots to cheer for in October! Including *yourself*. For all the things you've done—and all the great things you're going to do—three cheers for YOU!

1 _____ *5* _____

2 _____ *6* _____

3 _____ *7* _____

4 First man-made satellite launched by U.S.S.R., 1957   *8* Rev. Jesse Jackson born 1941

9 _____

10 _____

11 _____

12 Columbus Day_____

13 _____

14 National Friendship Day_____

15 _____

16 _____

17 _____

18 _____

19 _____

20 _____

21 _____

22 _____

23 _____

24 United Nations Day_____

25 _____

26 _____

27 _____

28 Statue of Liberty given to U.S., 1886_____

29 _____

30 _____

31 Halloween_____

WEEK 1
Tons of Talent

God's Amazing Word

*Now you are the body of Christ,
and each one of you is a part of it.*
I Corinthians 12:27 (NIV)

PEANUTS, POPCORN, PROJECTS

"Popcorn! Peanuts! Cotton candy!" the man yelled as he moved up and down the aisles of the coliseum. Far below, three huge rings shimmered in a swirl of colored light.

"Don't you just love the circus?" Holly asked, waving her elephant pennant.

"Uh-huh," Shawna said, her chin resting on her hand.

"Well, you certainly don't look like it!" Holly laughed.

Shawna sat up straighter. "I was just thinking about that history project for school."

"Your group's almost ready to present it to the class, isn't it?"

"Yeah. It's just that...well...." Shawna bit her lower lip. "It's not fair, Holly. It's just not fair!"

"What's not fair?"

"Everybody else in the group gets to do something fun. Jeff and Brett are going to pretend they're soldiers and reenact the

Battle of Bunker Hill. Amy's going to wear her grandma's long dress and be Betsy Ross, making the first flag."

"And what do you get to do?"

"I have to paint the Liberty Bell on this big piece of cardboard that goes behind the actors. I don't even get to be up front during the presentation! Why do I have to paint some stupid piece of cardboard when everyone else gets to wear a costume?"

"But Shawna, you're the best artist in the class. Your Liberty Bell will be super! The project wouldn't be nearly as good if your group had to perform in front of that ugly old chalkboard!"

"Ladies and gentlemen!" a deep voice boomed from big black speakers overhead. "Welcome to the *Greatest Show on Earth!*" The crowd burst into applause as a fanfare of music started.

"Oh, look!" Holly said. "Elephants!" The huge gray beasts thundered in, hanging onto each others' tails with their long trunks.

"And clowns," Shawna laughed.

It was a wonderful show! Lion tamers cracked their whips as the huge beasts jumped through flaming hoops. Vanilla-colored stallions danced on their hind legs.

"And now, ladies and gentlemen," the voice announced, "performing for your pleasure on the high wire, the amazing Flying Fetachillis!"

Suddenly, a cymbal crashed. Rays of colored lights swung across the center ring, glistening off the sequined costumes of six trapeze artists. They seemed to fly through the air, catching each other with split-second timing. When the performance ended, Holly and Shawna couldn't clap hard enough.

"No wonder they call it the *Greatest Show on Earth!*" Shawna said.

"It takes a lot of teamwork to do that trapeze routine!" Holly said.

Shawna nodded. "You need a lot of people to put on a good show."

"No kidding! Think about all the animal trainers and feeders, all the cooks and roustabouts and costume makers who never even get to take a bow."

Shawna did think about them. "They're important, too, aren't they?"

"You bet!" Holly pushed open the door, and the girls squinted into the bright sunshine.

"Come on," Shawna called, hurrying down the sidewalk. "I want to get home."

"What's the big rush?"

"I've got a Liberty Bell to paint," Shawna grinned. "It's my part of the 'Greatest *History Project* on Earth!'"

A Closer Look

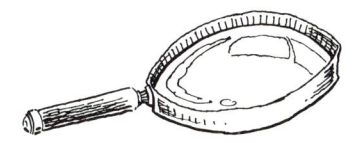

Sometimes being part of a team can be tough. Did you ever feel as though you got stuck with the worst job when family chores were assigned? Or that the coach made you sit on the bench too much? Or that what you had to do wasn't as exciting as what one of your classmates got to do?

Most of us feel that way at one time or another. But like links in a chain, we are each important. Equally important. We are all part of the body of Christ, but God has given us different talents. We can't all make field goals or play solos or get perfect spelling papers. But we can each do one thing—be a good team member!

What's Next?

What are some of the "teams" you're involved with? Maybe it's soccer or basketball. It could be a Scout troop or a church group. How about your family? Or even your neighborhood? Is there a project or job you need to work on together? A goal you can accomplish as a group? Probably! Determine right now to be a good team member, and make it official by signing your name on the medal below.

Fun Stuff

The circus is in town! Everyone is busy, trying to finish their activities in time to see the *Greatest Show on Earth*. But it will take lots of teamwork! Circle every example of teamwork in the picture on the next page.

(See Answer Page.)

Tell Me Another One

???Riddle???

Question: What has two heads and six legs?
Answer: A man on horseback!

The modern traveling circus began in 1768. It had only one attraction: a man balancing on horseback.

Those Amazing Animals!

Aren't elephants awesome? Here are some facts to prove it! Elephants can't jump. Even though they have the same number of bones in their feet as other animals do, an elephant's bones

17

are packed closely together. Because of this, they have none of the flexibility or "spring" that enables other animals to jump.

A full-grown elephant eats about four hundred pounds of food a day. If it lives in its natural jungle environment, it spends all its waking hours munching leaves, fruits, grasses, twigs and bark. But what does a zoo elephant eat? At the Bronx Zoo in New York, the elephants are fed three hundred pounds of hay, sixteen quarts of grain, and sixteen quarts of carrots, apples and stale Italian bread—every day!

From Me to God

Elephants are such wonderful, wrinkly creatures, God. Thanks for creating them—and all the other animals in the circus.

Thanks, too, for the special talents You've given me. Show me how to use them to be the best team member I can. At home, at church, at school, on the playing field—wherever I am!

★ ★ ★

WEEK 2
All Fired Up

God's Amazing Word

Be ready to do whatever is good....
Titus 3:1 (NIV)

FRENCH FRY FIASCO

"You sure you know how to make french fries?" Clevis asked, setting his books on the kitchen table.

"Sure I'm sure! I've watched my mom do it a hundred times." Mike reached inside the oven and pulled out a covered pan. "She keeps this grease just to use for french fries." He set the lid to one side and, placing the pan on the burner, turned on the fire.

"How long does it take for french fries?"

"You have to let the grease get real hot first," Mike said. "Let's make some chocolate milk while we wait."

The boys heaped big spoons of chocolate powder into their milk and began stirring. "What'd you think about that movie we saw in science today?" Clevis asked.

"I liked the part about Smokey the Bear, but the rest was boring."

"Boring? I thought it was pretty interesting stuff." Clevis stopped stirring his milk. "I might even become a fireman when I grow up."

"I can see you now," Mike laughed, "hanging onto the back of the fire truck as it speeds down the highway...."

"Hey, Mike! Look at the grease!" Dark swirls of smoke rose from the pan. "Is something wrong with it?"

"No," Mike said slowly. "I guess it's just hot, that's all." He reached into the freezer for the big bag of french fries. "I'll just drop in a few to see if it's ready." Using a long-handled spoon, Mike dropped a handful of potatoes into the pan. Grease splattered everywhere. And suddenly, little bursts of fire blazed on the top of the stove. "Oh, no!" Just then, the whole pan ignited in a bright flame. "Fire! It's a fire! Get some water!" Mike raced for the sink and began filling up a tall glass.

"No!" Clevis said, grabbing a hot mitt. "Don't put water on a grease fire. We have to smother it!" Quickly he lowered the lid onto the flames. Then he turned off the burner. Both boys stood staring at the pan.

"Suppose it's out?" Mike asked, his voice a bit shaky.

Clevis nodded. "Fire needs three things to burn: heat, air and fuel. The fire died because we took away its air by putting the lid on the pan."

"How'd you know that?"

"The same way I knew not to put water on a grease fire," Clevis grinned. "From watching that *boring* film!"

"You know," Mike said, "you'd make a good fireman."

"And you'd make a terrible cook!" Clevis laughed, holding up a burnt french fry.

A Closer Look

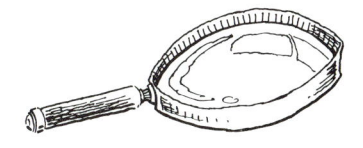

Do you ever feel as though the things you are learning at school have little to do with what's really happening in your life? The date Columbus discovered America, how many quarts in a gallon, the sounds of hard and soft *c*. Mike thought the movie was boring, just a bunch of facts that had nothing to do with him. But he was wrong! The information in the movie turned out to be important. Both boys were glad Clevis had paid attention, glad he was *prepared*.

Don't be too quick to close your mind to math facts or spelling lists or geography lessons. School is filled with things that get you ready for life, with lessons that prepare you for the challenges waiting for you tomorrow—maybe even *today*!

What's Next?

It's important to plan ahead, to be ready for emergencies. Would you know what to do if you woke to a fire in your house? Does your family have a plan of action in case of fire? Below are four THINGS TO REMEMBER. Read through this list. Then share it with two other people, at least one of whom is part of your family.

THINGS TO REMEMBER

1. Have home fire drills. Plan a special place outside to meet.

2. If there is smoke in a room, crawl low near the floor where the air is safer.

3. Never open a door that is warm to the touch.

4. If your clothes should catch on fire, don't panic! Remember this rule: STOP, DROP and ROLL. This will put out the flames.

☆   ☆   ☆

Fun Stuff

Fire has been around for a long, long time. But the first match was invented just one hundred sixty years ago. Every year, more than five *billion* matches are produced in the United States. Match factories pack them into boxes at the rate of a million matches an hour! Did you know that many fires are caused by careless use of matches, by children playing with these tiny flammable sticks? It's true! Two out of every ten fires start this way.

Circle every "hidden" match in the picture below. And remember—matches are tools, not *toys*! Never play with matches or lighters or open flames.

(See Answer Page.)

Those Amazing Animals!

Have you ever heard of Smokey the Bear? He's more than just a poster cartoon. There really was a Smokey!

In 1944, the U.S. Forest Service found a badly burned cub that had survived a fire in the Lincoln National Forest in New Mexico. They named him Smokey and made him spokesman for the outdoors and fire safety. When Smokey finally recovered from his burns, he went to live at the National Zoo in Washington, D.C. For many, many years he was a favorite of the kids and adults, too.

Smokey died on November 9, 1976—but his character lives on, teaching children the importance of "helping to prevent forest fires."

Tell Me Another One

The Chicago Fire of 1871 destroyed most of that great city. Rumor says that the blaze started when Mrs. O'Leary's cow kicked over a nearby lantern, but no one knows for sure. The Water Tower was one of the few buildings left standing after the fire.

From Me to God

Thanks, God, for the wonder of fire—to cook my food and keep me warm. I'm going to listen harder to the lessons all around me. That way I'll be ready for whatever comes. You'll help me, won't You? Thanks!

★ ★ ★

WEEK 3
Word Power

God's Amazing Word

> May the words of my mouth...
> be pleasing in your sight,
> O Lord....
>
> Psalm 19:14 (NIV)

MISSY'S MISTAKE

"She didn't *really* say that?" Amber asked, lacing up her tennis shoe.

"Yes, she did!" Missy said. "She said your mother treated you like a baby. And that every time she was over there she felt like she was back in nursery school."

"Well, she won't have to worry about it. I'm never inviting Sandi to my house again as long as I live!" Amber ran to get in line for gym class. Sandi got in line behind her.

"I hope we play kickball today," Sandi whispered.

Amber pretended not to hear.

"Hey, what's the matter with you?" Sandi asked.

"If certain people think I'm going to be friends with them after the terrible things they say, then certain people are wrong!" Amber said without turning around.

"What are you talking about?"

"You know," Amber said, turning to face her. "And I think your mother treats you like a baby, too!"

"All right, class," the teacher called. "Let's go to the gym. Straight line. No talking."

The girls walked in silence. Sandi got to be one of the kickball captains. Usually she chose Amber first, but today she didn't choose her at all.

After school, Amber hurried out to the bus and sat with Missy. When Sandi got on, they giggled. "There she is," Amber said, pointing.

Sandi deliberately knocked Amber's books onto the floor when she passed.

"Hey, you did that on purpose!" Amber yelled, but Sandi didn't even turn around.

The next day Missy was absent. Amber stood alone on the playground, watching the other kids climbing and sliding and playing tag. She looked across the yard and saw that Sandi was alone, too. *If only she hadn't said those mean things about my mom,* Amber thought. *We've been friends forever....*

Sandi began walking toward the swings. When she got close to where Amber was standing, she stopped. Neither girl spoke. Amber saw Sandi was wearing the hair barrettes she had given her for her birthday.

"Hi," Sandi said softly.

"Hi."

"Kind of cold today, huh?"

"Yeah."

Silence.

"How come you said those horrible things about my mom?" Amber blurted out. "And my house is not like a nursery school!"

"What horrible things? I have no idea what you're talking about!"

"Yes, you do! You said my mother treated me like a baby and that every time you came over you felt like you were back in nursery school."

"I did not!" Sandi said, her eyes wide. "I never, ever said that! Who told you I said that?"

Amber was quiet for a moment. "Missy."

"Missy? She's always trying to make trouble. You know that, Amber."

It was true. Missy was always tattling or starting rumors. "But why would she have made that up?"

Sandi shrugged. "Maybe because you always sit with me on the bus and play with me at recess."

Just then the whistle blew for the end of recess. "See you after school," Amber waved, running to get in line. She stopped and turned around. "Save me a seat on the bus?"

Sandi smiled. "Sure! What are friends for?"

A Closer Look

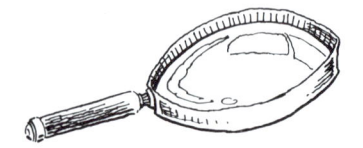

Have you ever noticed how powerful words are? They can make friends and break down walls of shyness. They can make people feel better—or worse. Because words are so strong, you need to be careful how you use them. Remember how awful Amber felt because of what Missy said? So before you repeat something, ask yourself these two questions: (1) Is it true? (2) Will it make this person feel happy? If the answer to both questions is "yes," then share your information. But if you aren't sure of your facts or if what you say might hurt someone's feelings, then stop. Make sure your words are the *happy* kind!

What's Next?

How do you feel when someone pays you a compliment? When your best friend likes your shirt or your teacher comments on how neat your science report is. Or your mother is pleased with the way your room looks. These things make you feel pretty good, don't they? Words have the power not only to *hurt*, as Missy's lies did, but also the power to *heal*. They can make a person feel happy and smart and pretty.

Think of someone who could use a kind word or two—a friend, relative, neighbor. Plan right now to give them a "gift" of good words. Fill in the blanks below—and then do it!

Something kind I can say to

_____
(person's name)

is

(good words)

☆   ☆   ☆

Fun Stuff

Some words are hiding in the puzzle below. Shade in the dotted areas to find out the answer. They're the two most important words you need after a fight with a friend.

(See Answer Page.)

Meet a Surprise Friend

Noah Webster loved words. And books. Born in 1758, he spent his childhood working on his father's farm. He did not have any books of his own. He read the family Bible and the *Ames Almanack*, a special book that told about weather prediction for the year. Noah longed for other books—books about stars and other countries, books of pirate stories and grammar lessons, books that would help him learn all about the world.

Eventually, Noah got his wish. A new minister moved into his West Hartford, Connecticut, community. He had lots of books, and he was eager to help Noah. When he was a teenager, Noah attended Yale University and became a teacher. He even wrote his own textbooks!

But he is best remembered for his greatest work, one that took him *fifty years* to complete! In 1828, Noah Webster published his *American Dictionary of the English Language*, the first book to define the speech of the people of the United States.

Wonderful Words

The United States is a mixture of people from all over the world—and our language shows it. Here are the origins of some of our borrowed words:

Hippopotamus comes from two Greek words—*hippo* and *potamos*. It means "river horse."

Lollypop has its beginnings in northern England. There the word *lolly* means "tongue." So a lump of candy that you "pop" in and out of your mouth and onto your tongue is a lollypop.

Muscle comes from the Latin *musculus*, which means "little mouse." If you flex and relax the muscles in your upper arm, it looks like a little mouse running under your skin.

From Me to God

Thanks for creating words, God. It sure would be hard to get along without them! I'll try hard this week to use my words to help and not hurt people.

★ ★ ★

Snappy Talk

FUN WITH WALLY

I JUST LOVE HALLOWEEN!

ALL THOSE DELICIOUS LITTLE CANDY BARS--

AND YUMMY PEANUT BUTTER KISSES!

SOMEHOW THIS WASN'T QUITE WHAT I HAD IN MIND...

WEEK 4
A Time to Believe in Yourself

God's Amazing Word

> *Let everyone be sure that he is doing his very best, for then he will have the personal satisfaction of work well done, and won't need to compare himself with someone else.*
>
> Galatians 6:4 (TLB)

ANTON'S DISCOVERY

Anton opened his eyes just as the sun was rising. He awoke with a sense of excitement, although at first he couldn't remember why. "The beasties!" he said, sitting up and pushing back the covers. "I must see if the beasties are still there!"

Anton van Leeuwenhoek had always been a keen observer. When he was just a boy learning the dry goods trade, one of his jobs was to look at the material under a magnifying glass. But every chance he got, Anton looked at other things with the magnifying glass, too.

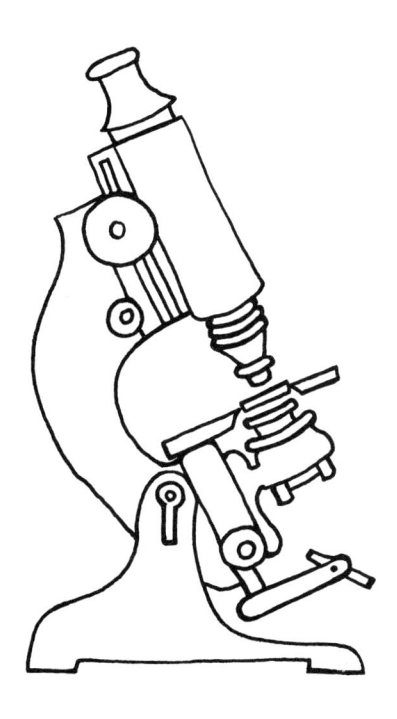

And later, when he was a man and had his own store, he learned how to grind lenses that would greatly enlarge things. This became his hobby, and he spent many hours looking at the legs of flies, the stingers of bees and the blood vessels in a fish's tail.

But last night—last night he had seen *something alive* under his microscope!

Anton hurried to the storeroom of his dry goods store. There, amid the bolts of cloth, were his lenses. He took a drop of water from a nearby pail and placed the glass close to his eye. "There they are!" he cried in amazement. "Millions of them, swarming like gnats! And a thousand times smaller than the eye of a louse!"

"Anton!" his wife called. "Come open the shop. Already customers are waiting outside!"

"I cannot come now. Tell them we are closed."

"And why are we closed?" his wife asked, standing in the doorway of the storeroom.

"Because," Anton laughed, "I have discovered a whole world—an invisible world!"

"Augh! That foolishness with the lenses again. This nonsense will be the ruin of us all. All of Holland will call you Anton van Leeuwenhoek—the dunce of Delft." She shook her head in disgust as she walked away.

Anton looked around. "Now where else might these beasties live, besides pond water?" He noticed a forgotten glass of milk sitting on his table. "Perhaps in stale milk...."

These "beasties," Anton would discover, lived in lots of places: in rotten meat and spoiling milk, in muddy puddles and in the tartar he scraped from his teeth. Even in human blood! It was a totally new idea for science in the 1600s—the possibility of unseen creatures living all around us.

Anton continued all of his life to build more microscopes and study this unseen world. He made drawings and kept careful notes. When he was forty years old, he sold his shop and devoted all his time to his research. When he died at the age of ninety-two, he was famous all over Europe for his discoveries. Called the "Father of the Microscope," Anton van Leeuwenhoek helped prepare the way for doctors and scientists to learn about bacteria and germs—and how to fight them.

A Closer Look

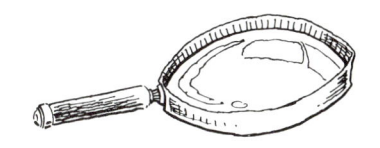

Did you ever work hard on a project—a rock collection or a short story or a piano piece—only to have someone tell you that you were wasting your time, that you would never succeed? That's what happened to Anton van Leeuwenhoek, too! But instead of giving up, he worked even harder. It's important to keep working for what you want, even when you don't get encouragement from your friends. Sometimes even your family. Look deep inside yourself, and if a particular goal is really important to you—if you want to walk on the moon or play second base for the Cubs or open on Broadway—then work and pray and work some more!

What's Next?

Think now of something out of the ordinary you'd like to try. Maybe it's oil painting or horeseback riding or *origami* (art of Japanese paper folding). Break out of your rut and be creative. Draw. Bake. Explore *yourself*. Be the very best you can be! On the line below, write one new thing you will try this month:

☆ ☆ ☆

Fun Stuff

Below are some giant germs. (Anton wouldn't have needed his microscope to see these!) On each one is a set of letters and a number. Copy the letters in order in the blanks on the next page to see what the message is.

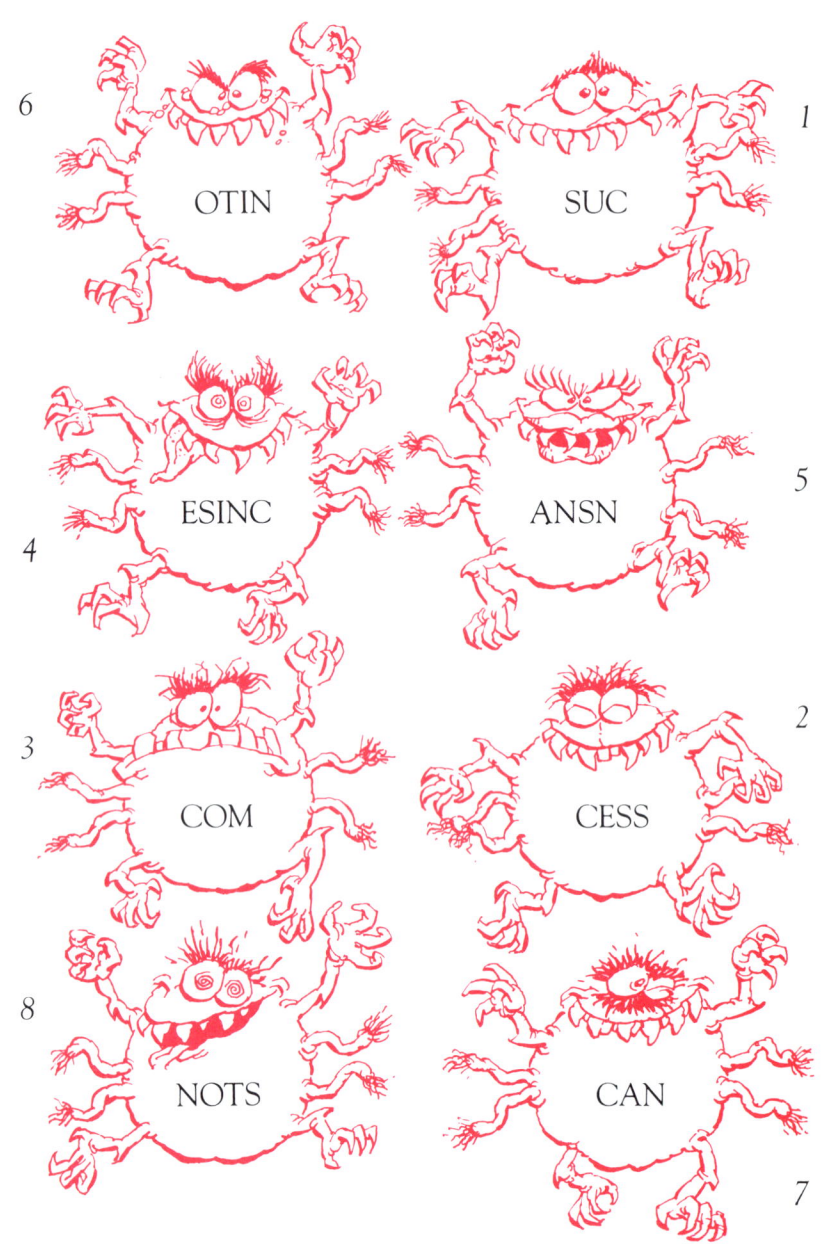

6 OTIN

1 SUC

4 ESINC

5 ANSN

3 COM

2 CESS

8 NOTS

7 CAN

___ __ __ __ __ __ __

__ __ __ __ __ __ __

__ __ __ __ , __ __ __

__ __ __ __ __ __ __ __ !

(See Answer Page.)

I Wonder Why?

Did you ever wonder why you see birds flying south as the weather gets cold? They're *migrating*. Animals migrate, move from one part of the world to another, for two main reasons. One is *breeding*. Some animals need special conditions so they can raise their young. The other reason is *feeding*. Often cold weather causes animals to move to warmer climates in search of food. By migrating between two parts of the world, animals get the best of both places. Birds are the most common migrants. But some insects, fish, whales and other land animals also travel when seasons change.

Those Amazing Animals!

Just how far can animals migrate? You might be surprised....

The Monarch butterfly travels two thousand miles, round-trip, from Canada to California.

41

The Atlantic salmon travels six thousand miles in the ocean, round-trip, from the St. Lawrence River to the Atlantic Ocean.

The humpback whale travels a total of eight thousand miles, round-trip, from the Indian Ocean to the Atlantic Ocean.

Wonderful Me

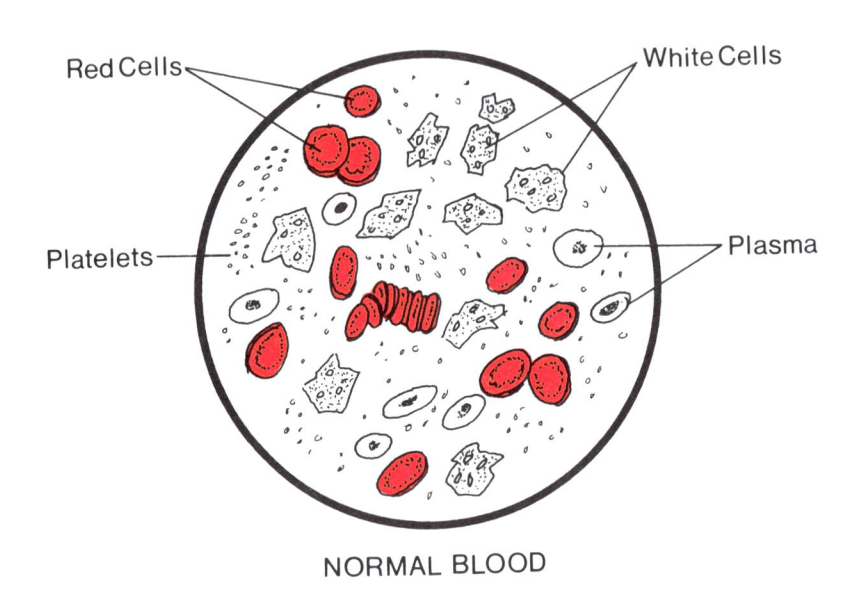

Red Cells • White Cells • Platelets • Plasma

NORMAL BLOOD

Have you ever looked at a drop of blood under a microscope? If you have, you saw more than just a blob of bright red fluid. Blood is made up of four elements: red blood cells, white blood cells, platelets and plasma. Red blood cells carry oxygen to various parts of your body. White blood cells fight off germs. Whenever you scrape your knee or cut your finger, it's the platelets that help your blood clot so the bleeding stops. Plasma is the fluid that holds it all together.

From Me to God

It's pretty amazing the way You created all the big things we can see—and all the little things we can't!

Sometimes, God, I'm afraid to try something new—afraid I'll fail. Whenever I feel that way, remind me that with Your help I can do great things! Thanks.

★ ★ ★

WEEK 5
Of Tricks and Treats

God's Amazing Word

Always be kind to everyone....
Galatians 6:10 (TLB)

AN UNEXPECTED TREAT

"Come on," Erin said, grabbing her "Happy Halloween" bag. "Let's get going before all the good candy is gone!"

"Almost ready. Can you help me with this last bit of straw?" Robbie asked.

"You look like a real scarecrow," Erin laughed, stuffing handfuls of straw up his sleeves.

"And how do I look?" Tara swirled around and waved her magic wand.

Erin eyed the blue sparkly dress and plastic-wrap wings.

"Definitely the best looking fairy godmother on the block. Now let's go!"

"We going to trick-or-treat Mr. Benson this year?" Robbie asked as they started down the steps.

"Are you kidding?" Tara asked. "I wouldn't go near that old place at night for four thousand candy bars! Just thinking about it gives me the creeps."

"My big brother says old man Benson keeps bats for pets and lets them all loose in his yard on Halloween," Erin whispered. "Besides, no kid has ever gotten a piece of candy from him!"

"Which way are we going?" Robbie asked as they reached the sidewalk.

"This way," Tara said, starting off down the street to her left.

"Why this way?"

"Because," Tara said, pointing over her shoulder, "Mr. Benson lives *that* way!"

Tara, Robbie and Erin were sitting on Tara's back porch steps. "What a haul we made last night!" Tara laughed, poking her hand deep into her full trick-or-treat bag.

"Yeah, it was great!" Erin said between licks on her lollypop.

"I'm still itching from that stupid straw!" Robbie tried to scratch the middle of his back.

"Let's go see what some of the other kids got," Tara said, grabbing her bag of candy.

The three kids started down the street. Before they realized it, they were in front of Mr. Benson's house.

"Look, he's out in the yard!" Tara whispered.

Mr. Benson was jabbing at his trees with an old broom. Toilet paper hung from every branch. His bushes, too, were covered with droopy tissue. A smashed pumpkin lay on his front porch. He looked cold and tired. And old. Suddenly he noticed the children. "Augh!" he said, waving the broom handle. "Come back to laugh at me, did you? To admire your work...."

"Hey," Robbie said, "we didn't do this!"

"Bah!" Mr. Benson put the broom down. "You're all alike. Vicious and mean." He went back to work, picking wet paper from his hedge.

"I'm going to help him," Robbie said.

"No, wait!" Tara said. But it was too late. Robbie had already pushed open the gate and was standing inside the yard. Mr. Benson whirled around to face him.

"I didn't do this, sir," Robbie said, swallowing hard. "But I'm going to help you clean it up." He picked up a nearby rake and began pulling strips of toilet paper from the low branches of the trees.

"And so are we!" Erin grabbed Tara's hand and pulled her up the walk.

Mr. Benson didn't speak. He just looked at the three of them with his cold, gray eyes and then went back to work.

Soon the yard looked perfect. Well, almost perfect. "Sorry we couldn't get those strips way high up," Robbie said as they all sat down on the steps to rest. The porch was still a little wet from where Tara had washed off the pieces of splattered pumpkin.

Mr. Benson stood beside them, as silent and grouchy as ever. He pushed his toe against Tara's Halloween bag. "'Happy Halloween.' Bah! I've never seen anything 'happy' about youngsters misbehavin' and stayin' out way past dark."

"But trick-or-treat is fun!" Erin said.

"Treat? All I've ever known is *tricks* on All Hallow's Eve. Nothing but tricks...." Mr. Benson looked around at his clean yard and at the kids sitting on his steps. He stopped talking and cleared his throat. A slow, almost-forgotten-how smile crept to his lips. "At least until now."

"Have some candy, Mr. Benson." Tara held up her bulging sack.

"No, I've got a better idea," Mr. Benson said, disappearing inside the house. In a flash he was back with a big bowl of Halloween treats—tiny candy bars and black-and-orange kisses and pieces of bubble gum and licorice suckers.

"Happy Halloween, young 'uns," Mr. Benson said, shyly passing the big bowl.

"Happy Halloween to you, too!" the kids laughed, filling their hands with candy.

And they couldn't help but notice that Mr. Benson was laughing, too.

A Closer Look

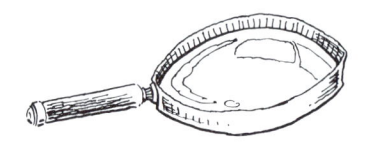

Have you ever known anyone who was shy and withdrawn, maybe even unfriendly? It's easy to suspect that such people are stuck up or, worse yet, just plain *bad*. But it isn't always that way. Sometimes they've been hurt by someone and have just built a shell around themselves. That's what Mr. Benson did. Or they may feel unsure and insecure, afraid that what they say or do won't be quite right. Often they're just too timid to make the first move toward friendship. So don't be too quick to believe rumors or judge people. It's almost *spooky* what great results a small offer of friendship can sometimes have!

What's Next?

Why not make a new friend this week? That quiet boy in your Sunday school class, the new girl in ballet, the shy older couple down the street. Plan something you can do together: bake pumpkin bread, carve a jack-o'-lantern, draw pictures to decorate your rooms, share a joke, talk on the phone. Let them know you are into "treating" them special!

☆   ☆   ☆

Fun Stuff

How do you feel when someone hurts your feelings? When you get to be first in line at recess? When your mom bakes your favorite cookies? *Emotions* are the way we feel about things. Here are some things that might happen to you. Match them with the pumpkin face that shows how you would feel in each situation: happy, scared, sad, mad, surprised.

1. You've been wanting a puppy for the longest time, and your dad brings home one for your birthday.

2. You hear a strange noise late at night.

3. Your puppy chewed up your homework.

4. Your best friend moves to another state.

5. Your cousin sneaks up behind you and yells, "BOO!"

(See Answer Page.)

Scared

Mad

Happy

Surprised

Sad

Now, on this blank pumpkin, draw the face that is your favorite—the one you plan on wearing this very day!

Wonderful Words

Have you ever heard the expression "blind as a bat"? Well, it's not exactly true! No normal, healthy bat is blind. Some, like fruit bats, have large eyes and good sight. But most bats have small eyes and rather poor sight. Does this make life difficult for them? Not at all! Most of their hunting is done in the darkness of night, when even the sharpest eyes are of little use. Their ears enable them to use a special "animal sonar." Bats find their prey by sending out high-pitched squeaks and listening for these to "bounce off" objects. *Squeak-Squeak. Beep-Beep.* Dinner!

Wonderful Me

Can you guess how many bones are in the human body? You don't have a *skeleton* of a chance without these clues:

Arm—32   Leg—31   Skull—29
Spine—26   Chest—25

So... how many bones are there in the human body?

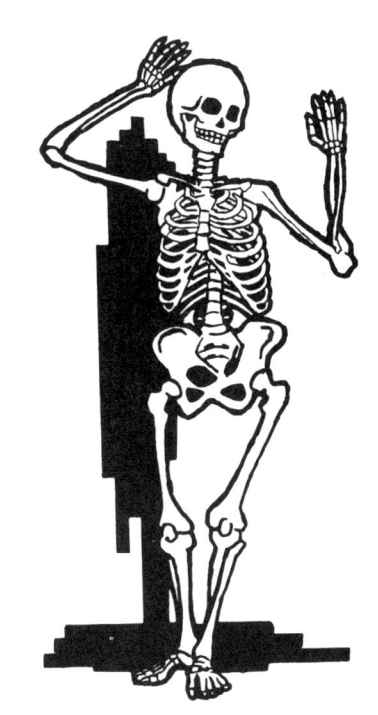

(See Answer Page.)

From Me to God

Thanks, God, for the special treats You send my way—friends and laughter and fun times. With Your help I'm going to be kind to everybody this week—especially those people who really need a friend!

★ ★ ★

Building a Better Me

How to Memorize Bible Verses

1. Did you know you can always have your Bible with you, whenever you need it? How? By memorizing Scripture! *Choose a verse that has special meaning to you.* John 3:16, Ephesians 4:32, Joshua 1:9 and Psalm 121:2 are good verses to begin with.

2. *Copy the verse on a piece of paper.* Writing will help you remember it. You may want to make a puzzle out of the verse by cutting the words apart and then trying to put them together in the right order. Keep trying!

3. *Place the verse where you can read it often.* Practice saying it aloud until the words and reference come easily to your mind. Know God will help you. He wants you to "hide" His word in your heart so that you will not sin against Him—that's what Psalm 119:11 says. Why not look up this verse and begin memorizing right now?

NOVEMBER

HALLELUJAH!

Thank you, Lord! How good you are! Your love for us continues on forever.

(Psalm 106:1, TLB)

Look around—what do you see? Bare trees, Pilgrim pictures, skies as gray as dishwater. But look closer—November is a good month really to look at everything you have to be thankful for… families, warm beds, wiggly pets…well, you can go on. Open your eyes to the blessings around you; open your heart to say, "Thanks, God!"

"FLOATING" HOLIDAY

Thanksgiving is always the fourth Thursday in November.

1 _____ *4* _____

2 _____ *5* _____

3 _____ *6* Adolphe Sax, inventor of saxophone, born 1814

7 _____

8 _____

9 _____

10 _____

11 Veterans Day _____

12 _____

13 _____

14 Dr. J. E. Branderberger invented cellophane, 1908

15 _____

16 _____

17 _____

18 _____

19 _____

20 _____

21 _____

22 _____

23 _____

24 _____

25 Joe DiMaggio born, 1914

26 _____

27 _____

28 First auto race in America, 1895

29 _____

30 _____

WEEK 6
Fall In!

God's Amazing Word

Do not follow the crowd in doing wrong.

Exodus 23:2 (NIV)

A MATTER OF HONOR

"I can't wait until tomorrow," Justin said, tossing the football to Brad.

"What's so special about tomorrow?" Brad asked.

Justin ran back for the catch. "It's the Veterans Day assembly at school. We get out of math and reading."

"That's right!"

"And this year the assembly won't be so boring."

The boys sat on the back steps of Brad's house. "I didn't think it was so bad last year. It's kind of neat to see all those soldiers dressed up in uniform and the color guard carrying the flag. And to hear the student council speeches about freedom and war. There's something kind of serious and special about the whole thing."

"This year's going to be *special* all right," Justin laughed. "But I wouldn't count on *serious*."

"What do you mean?"

He looked at Brad. "It's a secret. Nobody's supposed to know. Can you keep a secret?"

Brad shrugged. "Sure, I guess so."

Justin leaned closer. "Marv is bringing in a 'whoopee' cushion. When we all stand up for the Pledge of Allegiance, he's going to put it on Mr. Albert's seat. When he sits down—*whoosh-plat*! The whole place will die laughing. Pretty funny stuff, huh?"

"Yeah," Brad said slowly. "Real funny stuff."

The boys stood in line outside the auditorium. Justin kept looking at Brad and rolling his eyes. Marv had on his jean jacket. A funny bulge on the side let Brad know he had brought the whoopee cushion.

"This'll be great!" Justin whispered. "Half the kids won't notice until he sits on it—then Albert will get real red in the face and it'll be funnier than ever."

Brad didn't say anything.

The boys filed into the bleachers with the rest of their homeroom. Marv and Justin sat on the end of the row. Brad ended up near the middle. Mr. Albert brought in his students and sat down on the row in front of them, directly in front of Brad. Soon the bleachers were full, and the Veterans Day assembly began.

"Today we honor those veterans who have served in the Armed Forces," the principal said. "It is a solemn day, one set aside to show our thanks to the men and women who have fought and died for our country."

Brad looked at the rows of guests. Many of the men wore uniforms. Some had white hair. One soldier in particular caught Brad's attention. He was old and stooped. He sat in the front row, his uniform a leftover from some long-ago war. Stripes covered one sleeve.

Just then Marv and Justin broke out in giggles. Mr. Albert turned around and gave them his famous "be quiet or you're in big trouble" look.

"And now," the principal was saying, "let us recite the Pledge of Allegiance."

Everyone stood. The old soldier pulled himself erect. Brad could almost feel his pride as the flag was brought in. The old man had fought for that flag in some faraway place years and years ago....

Suddenly, Brad felt the boy next to him nudge him. "Here. Marv says to take this."

It was the whoopee cushion! He looked down the row. Marv and Justin pointed to Mr. Albert's seat. "Do it," they mouthed.

For an instant Brad held the cushion. He didn't want to play this stupid joke, but Marv and Justin were watching. Quickly, he laid the cushion on Mr. Albert's seat.

"... And to the Republic for which it stands...." Brad looked again at the old soldier. His eyes were on the flag. He was saying the words almost like a prayer. What would he think when all the kids started laughing?

"... With liberty and justice for all." With a last-minute swipe, Brad kicked the whoopee cushion on the floor just before Mr. Albert sat down. He heard coughing and looked down the row. Marv was mad. So was Justin. They were both glaring at him. "What'd you do that for?" Justin mouthed.

Brad looked away. He'd have to think of something to say to them. *Why did I do that?* he wondered as he kicked the whoopee cushion further under the bleachers. He watched the old soldier take one last look at the flag before he saluted it and sat down. *I did it for him*, Brad thought, smiling. *For him—and for me!*

A Closer Look

Have you ever been in a situation where your friends wanted you to do something you didn't think was quite right? Maybe it was copy answers to homework or throw rocks at pigeons or play pranks on the younger kids. It's hard to stand up for what you think is right. The *easy* thing is just to go along with the group—but often that's not the *right* thing. Brad knew the joke could ruin the Veterans Day assembly. He decided to do what he knew he should, not what Marv and Justin wanted him to do. So even if his friends hassle him, Brad can feel good about himself. And nothing feels better than that!

What's Next?

Patriotism is a word you often hear on the Fourth of July. It means "love of country." November 11, Veterans Day, is set aside to honor those who have served in the armed forces. Many of these people fought to keep America free; some of them even died. Do you know anyone who has been in the Army or Navy or Air Force? The Marines or Coast Guard or Reserves? Why not take a minute this week to thank him or her for helping make America "the land of the free and the home of the brave"?

☆ ☆ ☆

Fun Stuff

Knock, knock.
Who's there?
Leaf.
Leaf who?
Leaf your troubles behind
and have some fun with this
Fall Crossword Puzzle!

Fill in the puzzle with these things associated with autumn:

On Saturday, Brad woke up bright and early. Because it was a __1__ fall morning, there was __2__ on the ground. Mother wanted him to __3__ the __4__ , but he wanted to play __5__ . Brad put on a __6__ and went outside to work. Soon their yard was covered with piles of bright colors: __7__ , __8__ , and __9__ .

Brad's mother was so happy with the job he had done! She baked him a ___10___ pie and let him play with his friends the rest of the day.

(See Answer Page.)

I Wonder Why?

Did you ever wonder why leaves change color? Actually, the oranges and golds and reds you see in autumn have been in the leaves all along! But during spring and summer, when the leaves are making food, they produce a green substance called *chlorophyll*. The leaves are so full of chlorophyll that its green covers up the other colors. But just before cold weather, most trees stop making food and chlorophyll. So with the green gone, the other colors get their chance to be seen.

Tell Me Another One

Time out for some

FUN

Football

FACTS

The temperature was near zero that day in 1955 when Washington State College played San Jose State College. But did the cold weather discourage those hearty football fans? You better believe it! The game was played in front of only *one* paying customer.

There are losses and then there are *losses*.... In 1916, Georgia Tech's football team beat Cumberland University by an amazing score of 220 to 0.

From Me to God

Sometimes, God, when I'm with the other kids, I do things I really don't want to do—just to look cool. Forgive me. I want to do what's right, but it's so hard. Will You help me? Thanks!

★   ★   ★

WEEK 7
I'll Vote for That!

God's Amazing Word

Do not think of yourself more highly than you ought....

Romans 12:3 (NIV)

SEEING EYE TO EYE

Once upon a time, in the faraway and very hot kingdom of Guerktown, lived the Guerks. No clouds were allowed in Guerktown, and because the sun was always shining, the Guerks spent most of their time squinting. But they never wore anything to shade or cover their eyes, for everybody knew a Guerk's eyes were the most important thing about him. The Guerks were divided into two classes: the Browns and the Blues.

The Browns all had brown eyes and very dignified jobs. They lived in the best houses and attended the finest schools. They elected all the city officials and were the only ones allowed to attend the art galleries and concerts.

The Blues all had blue eyes. They lived in simple homes and had to work very hard. Since they were not permitted to attend school, they shared their knowledge with one other around campfires and kitchen tables. They could not vote.

Thus it had always been, and thus it probably would have been forever if it had not been for Baby.

Baby was born to the mayor and his wife—two of the brownest-eyed of the Browns. But, incredibly, Baby was born with one perfectly blue eye! What a predicament this presented! The village buzzed with the news. Baby could not possibly be a true Brown, but how could he be a Blue?

At last the town council met and decided that Baby would spend Mondays, Wednesdays, Fridays and Sundays with the

Browns. Tuesdays, Thursdays and Saturdays he would spend with the Blues. The council was sure that in a matter of weeks the true nature of the child would show through. Then he would be placed with his own kind.

But a remarkable thing happened. When Baby was with the Browns, he learned as quickly as any of them. And when he was with the Blues, he lifted the bales of straw high and laughed loudly at the antics of the farm animals. When he dressed in velvet, he ate with silver forks and had perfect table manners. When he wore burlap, Baby could toss a horseshoe as well as any of the Blues.

The town council met again. "This simply isn't working!" the oldest member said. "What shall we do?"

Shyly, a young councilman rose to his feet. "Is it possible," he asked, "that perhaps there isn't as much difference between the Browns and the Blues as we supposed?"

At first the council was stunned. But then they began whispering among themselves. "Yes," they murmured, "it is possible indeed!"

So things began to change in Guerktown. Browns could now be seen washing their own clothes; several bright Blues were studying to become doctors. Browns and Blues attended picnics and concerts together. The Blues showed the Browns how to repair leaky roofs. The Browns taught the Blues about Renaissance art. And every single Guerk turned out to vote in the next election.

Whatever happened to Baby? He became the richest Guerk of all. He invented a wonderful device called *sunglasses*. Soon every Guerk was wearing them and had stopped squinting—because everybody knew it didn't really matter what color your eyes were after all.

A Closer Look

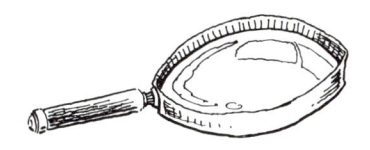

There are two parts to every person: the external and the internal. The external are the things about him or her you can see: his clothes, hair, bike, house, parents. The internal are the things you can't see, the things *inside*: her talents and fears, her faith and her dreams. Sometimes people decide another person's importance based on externals—the color of his skin or where he lives or what his mother does for a living. Or maybe even, like the Guerks, the color of his eyes. But it's really what's *inside* that counts— that makes everybody important!

What's Next?

Can you think of someone you know who seems different, somehow? Maybe he's shorter than the other boys in the class. Perhaps she wears clothes that don't fit quite right or has hair that hangs in her eyes. Or maybe he's just *too* smart. Why not make a special effort this week to be friendly to that person? You may find out they're not so very different after all!

Fun Stuff

This Guerk is trying to get to the polls to vote, but she's having a tough time. Can you help her?

(See Answer Page.)

Tell Me Another One

It's time for Election Day! On the first Tuesday after the first Monday in November, Americans eighteen years and older go to the polls and vote. Voting is done using a special lever in a ballot machine, listing all the candidates' names. By choosing councilmen and senators and school board members and presidents, voters have a say in their government.

Wonderful Words

Throughout the centuries, different objects have been used in voting. In Ancient Greece, men voted with colored stones. Black meant "no" and white meant "yes." Much of Colonial America voted using kernels of corn—different colors represented different opinions and choices. In 1888, a paper ballot listing the names of all those running for office was first used in the United States.

The word *ballot* was first used in Venice and Florence because colored balls, *ballotta*, were used for voting.

From Me to God

Sometimes, God, I decide whether or not I like somebody without really getting to know them. Forgive me. Teach me to look for the internal things. Remind me that You have made us all. Thanks!

★ ★ ★

Snappy Talk

FUN WITH WALLY

Panel 1: ANIMALS PREPARE FOR WINTER IN LOTS OF DIFFERENT WAYS.

Panel 2: BEARS SLEEP AWAY THE COLD MONTHS. ZZZZZZ

Panel 3: BIRDS FLY SOUTH.

Panel 4: AND I STOCK UP ON THE ESSENTIALS! PIZZA PIZZA PIZZA PIZZA PIZZA PIZZA PIZZA WALLY

71

WEEK 8
Pigeons and Pilgrims

God's Amazing Word

What I [God] want from you is your true thanks....

Psalm 50:14 (TLB)

SOMETHING TO BE THANKFUL FOR

"I can't wait till tomorrow. All my cousins from Atlanta are coming over for Thanksgiving dinner!"

"My mama's making the biggest turkey in Georgia! And you should see the pies...."

Thomas Earl lagged behind the other children. He didn't want to hear about their Thanksgiving plans. He didn't want to hear about turkeys and families and pumpkin pies. "I wish Thanksgiving had never been invented!" he mumbled to himself, sinking into the back seat of the bus for the long ride home.

Grandma was waiting for him at the bus stop, a brown grocery bag in her arms. "Well, boy, how was school?" she asked.

"Fine."

"Learn somethin'?"

"Yes, ma'am."

"Good!" They walked in silence. "Know what I got in this here bag, Thomas Earl? Thanksgiving dinner. Yes sir, tomorrow's a special day. Day to thank God."

Thomas Earl looked at the small sack. There was no turkey hidden there. Or pumpkin pie. And their tiny apartment would not be filled with family, laughing and eager to share Thanksgiving dinner. Only the two of them.

"How you like your Thanksgiving dinner, boy?" Grandma asked, popping a forkful of stuffing into her mouth.

"It's good, Grams," Thomas Earl said, poking at his chicken leg.

"Eat those peas. Green stuff makes you grow."

Thomas Earl stuck his fork into five peas, pretending they were sweet potatoes smothered in marshmallows and brown sugar.

"Dessert's special today," Grandma said, pushing back her chair and going to the refrigerator. From the freezer she took two tiny cups of ice cream. Fudge was swirled on the top of each. "I recall you always loved these when you was little. Called them 'ice cream Mondays,' remember?" Grandma chuckled.

Thomas Earl smiled. "Yeah, I remember."

When dinner was over, Thomas Earl helped wash the dishes.

"And now, it's time to feed the guests," Grandma said.

"Guests? What guests?"

Grandma winked. "Got to have guests on Thanksgiving! Get your coat and gloves on. We have to go to where these guests are."

Quickly, Thomas Earl got ready. Where could they be going? What kind of guests couldn't come to them? Grandma was waiting for him at the door, a brown bundle under her arm. The day was crisp and clear, with the clean smell of frost and turning leaves. Together they walked to the park.

"What are we doing here?" Thomas Earl asked, burying his hands in his pockets.

"Feeding our Thanksgiving guests," she said matter-of-factly, pulling a big loaf of bread from the bundle. She broke off a piece and threw it toward a group of pigeons. They gobbled it greedily. She tossed them another and another, each piece bringing them closer. "You help, too."

Thomas Earl took a handful of bread and began tearing it into little pieces, tossing it to the silvery birds. "They sure are hungry," he said. "Hey, I'm surrounded!" he laughed as the birds flocked around him, waiting for the next scrap of bread.

"These here are God's creatures, Thomas Earl, and our guests. We ain't got much, but we got full bellies and each other. We got these here pigeons to feed. God is good, boy. And don't you forget it."

Thomas Earl looked at his grandma. Her hands were bent from years of hard work; her face was covered with wrinkles. But she was full of life and love. She knew that Thanksgiving was more than fancy meals and lots of people. And now Thomas Earl knew, too. "No ma'am," he smiled. "I won't forget it."

They tossed out the last of the bread. "Let's play the 'Thank-you' game," Grandma said. "I'll start. I'm thankful for asters that bloom in my flower garden."

"I'm thankful for baseballs to throw."

"I'm thankful for chickens to eat on Thanksgiving." They kept taking turns, each naming, in alphabetical order, something they were thankful for.

It was Thomas Earl's turn to do *F*. He bent down and picked up a feather lying beside the path. "I'm thankful for feathers—and for the fine time we had today. Happy Thanksgiving, Grams."

"Happy Thanksgiving, boy," she smiled.

Then Thomas Earl and his grandmother turned down the alley toward home, leaving their full guests strutting contentedly in the park.

A Closer Look

Did you ever have one of those days when everything seemed to go wrong? You forgot your homework, the dog wet on your bedspread, your little sister ruined your favorite tape. Sometimes it's tough to find things to be thankful for—but they're always there, if you look hard enough. Thomas Earl was so busy looking at the things he *didn't* have that he couldn't see the things he *did* have! Why not make every day a *thanks-giving* day?

What's Next?

Have you ever played the "Thank-you" game? If not, this is a perfect time to start. Why not get a friend or family member to play along with you? The rules are simple: Go through the alphabet and name something you're thankful for that begins with each letter. Here are a few to get you started....

I AM THANKFUL FOR

A _____

B _____

C _____

D _____

E _____

F _____

☆ ☆ ☆

Fun Stuff

Use the words below to solve this "Pilgrim Puzzle." If you do every line correctly, the center blocks will spell out a very special day for the Pilgrims—and for you!

England	worship	Great
God	turkey	pumpkin
Bradford	friends	work
hard	corn	Virginia

1. The Pilgrims served _____ at their first feast.

2. That first year in the New World was _____ for the Pilgrims.

3. Gov. _____ issued the first Thanksgiving Day proclamation.

4. Squanto showed the Pilgrims how to plant _____.

5. The Pilgrims had to _____ so they would have a good crop.

6. The Pilgrims wanted to _____ God in their own way.

7. The Indians called God the _____ Spirit.

8. The Pilgrims invited their Indian _____ to the first Thanksgiving.

9. When the Pilgrims set sail in the Mayflower, they were trying to reach the colony of _____.

10. Lots of people eat _____ pie on Thanksgiving.

11. The Pilgrims sailed from _____ in search of religious freedom.

12. The Pilgrims gave thanks to _____—and so should we!

78

1. __ __ __
2. __ __ __
3. __ __ __ __
4. __ __ __ __
5. __ __ __ __
6. __ __ __ __
7. __ __ __
8. __ __ __ __
9. __ __ __ __ __
__ __ __ __ 10. __
11. __ __ __
12. __ __

(See Answer Page.)

79

Tell Me Another One

What goes *bounce, bounce, bounce?* No, it's not a basketball forward going in for a lay-up shot. It's a cranberry! All cranberries grown for sale undergo a "bounce test." Machines drop them six inches onto a board, and the berries bounce toward a barrier about three inches high. Fresh berries bounce right over. Spoiled berries don't. A berry gets seven chances to pass the test. If it doesn't, it never makes it to the Thanksgiving table.

I Wonder Why?

The Pilgrims got their first taste of popcorn when Quadequina, son of Massasoit, prepared some for them. Did you ever wonder why popcorn pops? Popcorn is different from other kinds of corn. Its kernels have a tough, waterproof covering that keeps the natural moisture inside the corn from escaping. When the kernels are heated enough, this moisture turns to steam and explodes the kernels.

From Me to God

Thanks, God, for all the good things—my family and pets, a warm house and good food, books to read and games to play and phones to call my friends. Thanks for all Your love and help. And thanks for Thanksgiving vacation from school!

★ ★ ★

WEEK 9
I Think I Can... I Think I Can

God's Amazing Word

Do not be afraid; do not be discouraged.
Deuteronomy 31:8 (NIV)

WRITE ON!

Ambrose sat on his bed, poking his pencil through the holes in his spiral. He opened to a clean page and tried to think of something to write. "Why did Mr. Emlet have to give us such a hard assignment? I'll never get this story done!" he said, tossing his notebook on the floor.

And that's when he noticed it. Shining out from under his closet door was a strange green light. A soft humming noise was coming from behind the door.

"Who's th-th-there?" Ambrose stammered. The humming stopped.

"Open the door and see," a voice said.

Slowly, Ambrose opened the door. Standing there was the strangest creature he'd ever seen. He was dressed all in white, and his long hair was covered with twinkling stars. He was barely tall enough to look Ambrose in the eye. "Who I am is not nearly so important as why I have come," he said.

"Why *have* you come?" Ambrose asked, stepping closer.

"To bring you this." He handed Ambrose a bright green pencil whose body was made of shimmering glitter. It had a flawless black point and a perfect pink eraser.

"Wow!" Ambrose said, turning the pencil over and over. "Awesome!"

"Yes," said the creature. "It is rather awesome. But it is also useful. You see, this pencil will enable you to write."

"Write what?"

"Why, anything you want! Stories and poems and reports and letters to your cousin Lance in Alaska. The pencil is yours for one month. Then I shall return for it." Suddenly, in a swirl of stardust, he was gone.

Ambrose stood gazing into the empty closet. "A magic pencil? Well, let's give it a try!" He picked up his spiral and thought for a moment. "Jeff had no idea it would be so dark," he wrote. "Cobwebs stuck to his cheeks as he struggled toward the tiny window at the far end of the attic...." By the time his aunt called him for supper, Ambrose had almost finished his story. "I can really write! It *is* magic!" he laughed.

It was a wonderful month. Ambrose finished his story, and Mr. Emlet liked it so much he put it up for everybody to read. Ambrose tried a few poems, too. And a mystery. He even joined the school newspaper staff.

Then one night, when Ambrose was busy writing a new science fiction story, he noticed that the strange light was back. So was the humming. Slowly, Ambrose opened the closet door. "Hi," he said, hiding the pencil behind his back.

"Hi to you," the creature said. "I have come for the pencil."

"Yeah, well, I lost it. On the way to school. It rolled into the gutter and...."

"It is behind your back at this very moment," the creature said simply.

"Okay, okay!" Ambrose said. "But I want to keep it. Look at all this great stuff I've written with it!" He showed him the story and poems, his mystery and a copy of the school newspaper. "And now I'm working on this story where an alien comes to earth disguised as a hamburger. I just have to keep this magic pencil!"

The creature laughed, and starlight danced around the room. "Now, human, I shall tell you the truth. The magic does not lie within the pencil."

"What do you mean?"

"The magic lies within *you*. You have been able to write these wonderful pieces because you *believed* you could. And that belief gave you the courage to work."

"Are you sure?"

"Absolutely." The creature reached for the pencil.

"You mean," Ambrose asked, handing it to him, "it was really me all the time?"

"All the time." The creature was silent for a moment. "Would you like to keep this, earthling? As a—what do you call it—souvenir?"

Ambrose looked at his half-finished story. "No, thanks," he smiled. "Take it to some other kid who needs a little 'magic.' I think from now on my yellow number 2 will be just fine!"

And in a sudden swirl of stardust, creature—and pencil—were gone.

A Closer Look

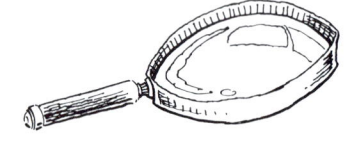

Have you ever wished for a little "magic" help? Maybe a magic basketball that always *swished* through the hoop. Or a violin that never squeaked. Or a piece of paper that corrected every misspelled word. Ambrose thought his successes were because of his "magic" pencil, but they really weren't. He succeeded because he believed in himself, because he refused to give up. And God is always ready to help you when you try to help yourself! Self-confidence—combined with hard work—can have wonderful, *magical* results.

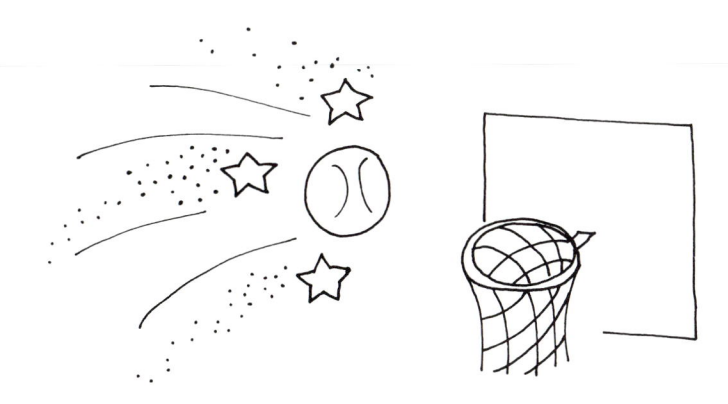

What's Next?

Is there something you've been dreading, something you feel you just can't do? That's how Ambrose felt about his writing assignment. But once he felt he *could do it*, everything changed! On the line below, write something that you must do. Maybe it's a science assignment or a band concert or an art project.

_____

Now, close your eyes and *see* yourself doing it—and doing it well. Carry that picture with you in your mind as you work to make it really happen.

Fun Stuff

Clarence thinks books are really "food for thought"! He has an important message for you. To find out what it is, write the letter that comes *before* each letter on the books. Copy the letters, in order, in the blanks on the next page.

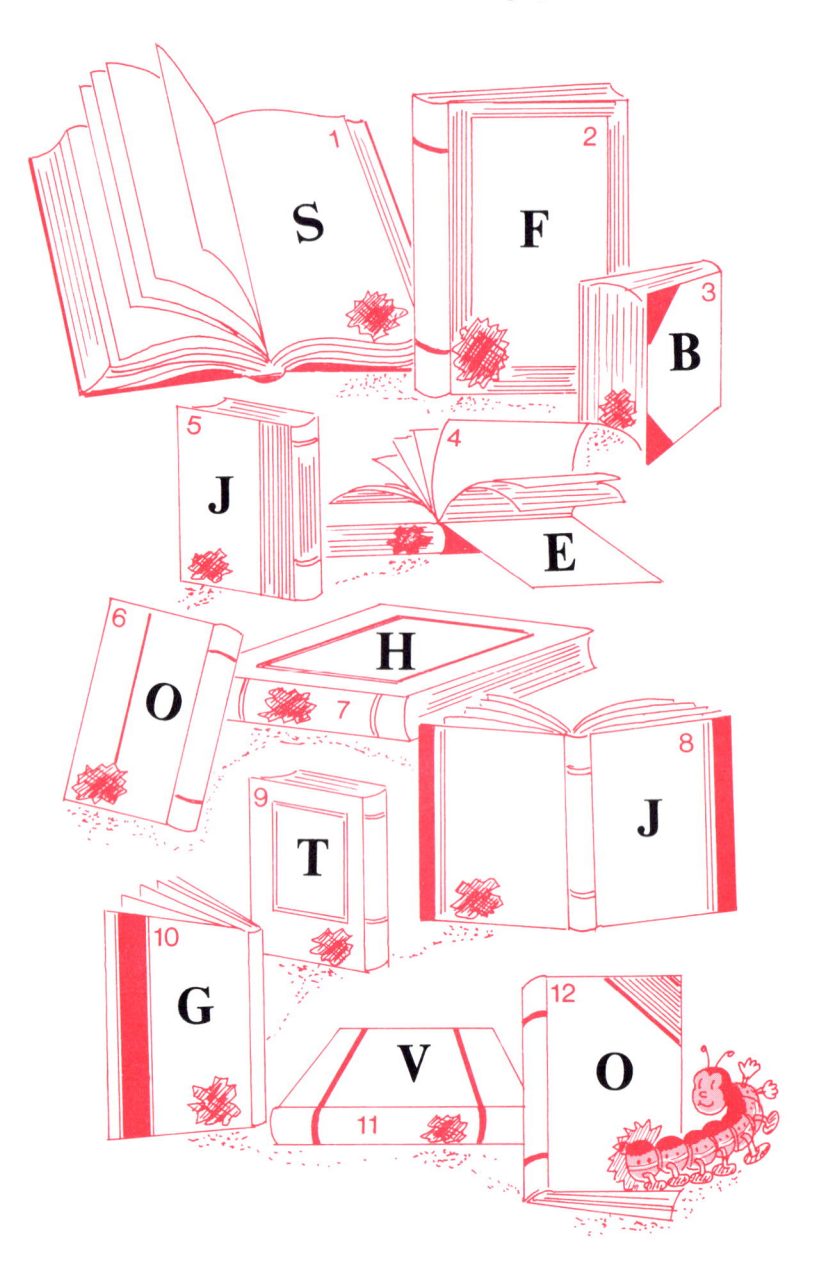

$\underline{}\ \underline{}\ \underline{}\ \underline{}\ \underline{}\ \underline{}\ \underline{}$
 1   2   3   4   5   6   7

$\underline{}\ \underline{}\quad \underline{}\ \underline{}\ \underline{}$!
 8   9   10   11   12

(See Answer Page.)

???RIDDLE???

Knock, knock.
Who's there?
Moe.
Moe who?
Moe fun and adventure—
It's easy to find.
All you need do is
To open your mind
And let in some friends
You have overlooked—
Friends who are waiting
Inside a good book!

CHECK IT OUT!

Tell Me Another One

Every November the Children's Book Council sponsors "Children's Book Week." This is a special time for kids just like you to celebrate books: the wonderful way they take you to far-away places, the useful things they teach you, the magic they bring to your block. Why not visit your public library sometime soon and e-x-p-a-n-d your mind?

From Me to God

Dear God, on those days when I feel as if I can't do anything right, remind me that I've got the "Super-natural" on my side. Knowing You're there to help me is magic enough. Thanks!

★ ★ ★

Building a Better Me

How to Handle Anger

1. Has anyone ever done anything that made you really mad? Maybe they cut in front of you in lunch line or tripped you on the playground. Do your parents ever tell you "no" when you want to stay up late or go somewhere with your friends? Has your little brother ever wrecked your bike? Everyone gets angry once in a while! It's how you handle your anger that's important.

2. Let the person who angers you know you're upset. Don't keep it inside. Try to speak calmly, telling him or her exactly why you are annoyed. Perhaps there's a good explanation for what happened; be prepared to listen. Ephesians 4:26 says, "If you are angry, don't sin by nursing your grudge" (TLB). Face up to the problem right away. And always be willing to forgive!

3. When you become angry, certain chemical changes occur in your body. You feel restless, full of energy. Sometimes a brisk bike ride, a run around the block, or even practicing a few lay-up shots can make you feel better.

DECEMBER

Holly and tinsel and
   shiny bright balls,
Pageant rehearsals
   and trips to the mall.
Singing old carols
   in soft candlelight,
Knowing the Christ Child
   was born on this night.
Sweet giggled secrets
   that no one can hear—
All these make Christmas
   the *best* time of year!

   Is Christmas an exciting time around your house? Do you sing carols, bake cookies and make bows, hang lights and lick envelopes? Most of all, do you celebrate God's gift to you—His gift of life and laughter and love? And the greatest gift of them all, the gift of God's Son.
   Have a happy, holy holiday!

1 _____

2 _____

3 First human heart transplant, 1967

4 _____

5 _____

6 _____

7 _____

8 _____

9 _____

10 _____

11 _____

12 _____

13 _____

14 _____

15 _____

16 Ludwig von Beethoven born, 1775

17 _____

18 _____

19 _____

20 _____

21 Winter begins

22 _____

23 _____

24 _____

25 Christmas Day

26 _____

27 _____

28 Chewing gum invented by American, William Semple, 1869

29 _____

30 _____

31 New Year's Eve

WEEK 10
Wings and Things

God's Amazing Word

God loves a cheerful giver.
II Corinthians 9:7 (NIV)

MOUNTAIN MAGIC

Fred couldn't keep his eyes off the clock. How could twenty minutes pass so slowly! He glanced again at the Christmas tree and the pile of presents under it.

"All right, class," Mrs. Rosetti said, "you may put away your books now."

It was time for the party!

"I'm gonna get that great big box," Bronko whispered, leaning across the aisle. "I saw David bring it in—and you know how rich he is. It could be anything!"

"Yeah," Fred said, looking at the presents. "You never know

what you'll get in these exchanges. Remember the year I got that giant jar of bubbles?" Both boys laughed.

"Now," said the teacher, shaking a small box with slips of paper in it, "every gift has a number taped on it. The number you choose is the present you get. After you find your present, take it to your seat. We'll open them all at the same time. You first, Angelo."

One by one the children pulled numbers out of the small box; one by one the presents disappeared from under the tree. Every time the huge present was still left, Bronko whispered an excited "Yes!"

Finally, only two people were left to draw: Fred and Bronko. Only two presents were left under the tree: the big one and a tiny one.

"I hope I don't get that shrimpy one!" Bronko whispered. "Hillbilly Henry brought that one in. My dad says his whole family's crazy, that they mess with 'mountain magic.' Henry probably wrapped up some magic dandelion stems...."

"Your turn, Bronko," Mrs. Rosetti said.

"Come on," Bronko whispered, closing his eyes and choosing a slip of paper. "Fourteen." He turned toward the tree. "Yes!" he said, reaching for the big box.

"Too bad for you!" he laughed as he passed Fred's desk.

Fred went to the front of the room, drew his slip and picked up the tiny package. It was wrapped in plain paper and tied with string.

"Okay," Mrs. Rosetti smiled, "you can open them!"

Squeals and giggles mixed with the tearing of paper. "Look what I got!" "Wow! A model plane!" "Barbie clothes!" "New crayons!"

Slowly Fred slid off the string and opened the box. He noticed that Henry was watching him from across the room. *No matter what it is*, he thought to himself, *I'm going to act as if I like it.* Inside was a piece of paper, folded several times. He unfolded it and read: *Look in the closet.* He glanced toward Henry, but he was busy opening his own gift. Fred walked to the front of the room. Slowly he opened the closet door. There, on the floor, was a butterfly collection. Bright wings splashed with yellow and black and purple were pinned to a big board.

"Go on, take it. It's yours." Henry was standing beside him.

"It's beautiful!" Fred said, lifting the board. "Where did you ever find it?"

"Shucks, I didn't find it—I made it!" Henry said. "Spent all summer collecting these. This here's a monarch," he said, touching the frail wing. "Found him out by the back pasture."

"It's a great present!" Fred thought about all the hours Henry had spent finding and mounting these specimens. "Sure you want to give it away?"

Henry laughed. "Sure I'm sure. *Giving* is what Christmas is all about!"

"What you got there?" Bronko asked, holding a new soccer ball. He looked over Fred's shoulder.

"A butterfly collection."

"A real one?"

"The genuine article," Henry beamed.

"Wow!" Bronko bent closer. Suddenly he stood up, a confused look on his face. "But how'd it fit in such a small box?"

"Mountain magic," Fred said, smiling at Henry. "Pure mountain magic!"

A Closer Look

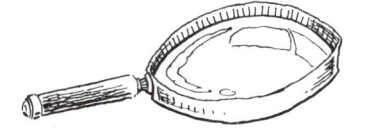

It's fun to get presents, isn't it? And exchanges with friends can be lots of fun. But when it comes to gifts, *bigger* doesn't always mean *better*. Bronko found that out! A great gift doesn't have to cost a lot of money or be big and fancy. A great gift is one that shows imagination and time and caring. Like Henry's butterfly collection. So don't be fooled by the size of a present. Good things can come in small packages!

What's Next?

What made Henry's gift special was that it was a real part of him. He had worked hard to collect and mount all those butterflies. His present for the class exchange had taken time and love and patience to prepare. Surprise someone this week with a unique gift—bake some cookies, draw a picture, write a poem, dabble in fingerpaints. Let your present be *you*-nique!

☆   ☆   ☆

Fun Stuff

Color the spaces with the letters *P, B, D,* and *W* with a pencil. Then copy the letters that remain into the blanks beneath the tree for a special Christmas message.

_ _

_ !

(See Answer Page.)

Meet a Surprise Friend

Did you know that there really was a St. Nicholas? A long time ago, about three hundred years after Jesus was born, he lived in part of what is now Turkey. He was the bishop of Myra. Although not much is known about him, legend has it that he loved children and gave them presents.

Nicholas became a popular saint, especially in Europe. When the Dutch colonists moved to North America, they brought their legends about St. Nicholas with them. They called him *Sinterklaas*—and from this comes our "Santa Claus."

From Me to God

I've been thinking a lot lately about the presents I'll be getting. But this week I'm going to think about giving, too. I know that's what Christmas is really all about!

★ ★ ★

WEEK 11
Not to Be Taken Lightly

God's Amazing Word

> *You are the light of the world...*
> *let your light shine before men,*
> *that they may see your good deeds*
> *and praise your Father in heaven.*
>
> Matthew 5:14,16 (NIV)

SERENDIPITY

"Did you see that kid yesterday?" Betty Ball said, her glow becoming even redder. "He almost dropped me!"

"We're sure to be bought soon," the stuffed Santa next to her said. "It's almost Christmas!"

"Know what happens if no one buys you before Christmas?" a pointed-eared elf asked, his voice deep and scary. "They slap one of those ugly 'half-price' stickers on you. Then some bargain hunter grabs you and sticks you up in a hot attic for a whole year. Sometimes they forget all about you—and you stay there forever!"

Serendipity tried not to listen. She tried not to think about the fact that all the other electric candles had already been bought. Of course, they had been matched sets with bright orange bulbs and tall white bodies. "I'm just a tiny thing," she sighed. "Who would want my puny light?"

Just then the store opened. Shoppers hurried down the aisles, clutching shopping lists. Overhead, Christmas carols played. Serendipity rustled against her plastic package and tried to look tall.

It was close to closing time when the old lady came in. She wore a dark blue coat and thick, black shoes. She walked slowly down the ornament aisle, fingering fuzzy poinsettias and glittery bells. She stopped directly in front of Serendipity. "What a lovely little candle!" she said. "And just the right size for my apartment window." Serendipity felt the old lady's hands around her, and then they were moving toward the check-out registers.

I'm being bought! Serendipity thought, her bulb pounding with happiness.

The old lady's apartment was small and lonely and dark. It had one window that faced the street below. She plugged in Serendipity as soon as they got home. How good it felt to glow after all those long nights sitting on the department store shelf! "I'll put you here in the window," she said, placing the candle on the ledge. "And these pieces of pine will make you look real Christmasy." Serendipity could smell the spicy sweetness of evergreens placed around her.

So Serendipity shone. Her brightness broke through the darkness pressing on the window, pushed back the shadows lurking in the room. Every morning the old lady would unplug her, and Serendipity would get some much needed rest. But from dusk to dawn—all night, every night—Serendipity's light gleamed in the window. And slowly, after a few days, strange and wonderful things began to happen.

"Just stopped in to wish you a Merry Christmas!" the neighbors from across the street said, stamping snow on the rug. "We saw your light in the window...."

"How about some cookies and cocoa?" the old lady asked as the visitors stepped into the warmth of the tiny room.

The next day, just as the blue darkness began to fall, someone knocked on the door again. It was the children from downstairs. "Are you real busy?" the older one asked shyly. "We saw your candle on our way home from school and thought you might have time to help us with our letters to Santa."

"Come in, come in!" the old lady laughed.

Twice that week carolers stopped underneath the window to sing. The old lady waved and Serendipity blinked.

All too soon, the holidays were over. The pine pieces around Serendipity were yellow and dry. Gently, the old lady carried them to the trash. "Well, little candle, it's time to pack away Christmas lights." She unplugged Serendipity. Power drained from her cord. Her bulb felt suddenly cold. The old lady stood looking out her tiny window at the gray sky. Slowly, a smile began turning up the corners of her mouth. "But 'welcome lights,' well... that's another matter." She plugged Serendipity in again. "And that's what you are. My 'welcome light.' To welcome neighbors and children and friends." Serendipity stood up straight and beamed her brightest.

So Serendipity and the old lady lived happily ever after, filling each other's lives with light and love.

A Closer Look

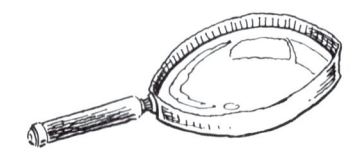

Christmas is a time for reaching out to other people—in big and little ways. Cards and packages, phone calls and surprise visits. A shoveled walk, a loaf of warm bread, an after-school hour spent listening to long-ago memories. Remember how Serendipity and the old lady *needed* each other? Well, we all need each other, too. That's a good thing to remember, at Christmas and always!

What's Next?

How busy the holiday season can be! Pageant rehearsals and shopping, making bows and baking cookies, whispered secrets and endless lists. Sometimes we get so busy with *things* that we forget to take time for *people*. Plan to spend a few minutes this week with a special person in your life—your grandma or mom, a friend or cousin, your pastor or priest. Share with them what you like best about Christmas—and listen to their "favorites," too.

☆   ☆   ☆

Meet a Surprise Friend

Did you know that Americans exchange more than two billion Christmas cards every year? Many of those cards have the word *Hallmark* on the back. "Hallmark Cards" is the dream-come-true of Joyce C. Hall.

Joyce Hall was always interested in cards. In 1907, when he was only sixteen years old, Joyce went into business with his two older brothers. They sold picture postcards. But as the years went by, Joyce began to feel that people wanted something more personal than postcards. His other brothers joined the company, now called the Hall Brothers, and they began printing original Christmas cards. As their cards became known for their quality and originality, business grew. In 1954 the name of the company was officially changed to Hallmark Cards, Inc.

Today, the company has a creative staff of close to one thousand people. They create over twenty thousand new designs each year. And every day they produce more than eleven million cards!

Fun Stuff

Here's your chance to write and design an original, one-of-a-kind Christmas card for someone special. Ready?

Don't you love sorting through cookbooks for fudge cookies

or yummy candy recipes? But did you know that poems can have "recipes," too? Here is a "recipe" for a four-line Christmas poem:

Line 1—Three words that describe Christmas
Line 2—Two "ing" words
Line 3—Sentence or group of words
Line 4—Christmas greeting

It's easier than it looks! (And you can't burn it or put in too much sugar or forget to stir it.) Here's a sample to show you how:

CHRISTMAS
Busy, bright, fun
Sparkling, bustling
My favorite time of year
Happy Holidays!

Now try your own four-line poem on the lines below. Use the "recipe" above, or create your own.

Copy your original poem on paper, illustrate it with Christmas borders or pictures, and mail (or hand deliver) this custom-made card to a special friend or relative. (Who knows—maybe Joyce C. Hall started out just like this!)

Wonderful Words

Did you ever wonder why Christmas songs are called carols? The word *carol* means "circle dance." Long ago, caroling was common at village festivals. People would dance arm-in-arm, singing happy songs with simple, beautiful melodies. Carols became one of the ways Christians expressed their joy at Christmas.

Because he encouraged the singing of Christmas carols, St. Francis of Assisi is sometimes called the Father of the Christmas Carol.

From Me to God

Christmas sure is great, God! Thanks for bright lights and big bows and snow as white as powdered sugar. Thanks for people who love me—and people I get to love back!

★ ★ ★

Snappy Talk

FUN WITH WALLY

WEEK 12
My Very Best

God's Amazing Word

> She [Mary] gave birth
> to her firstborn, a son...
> and placed him in a manger,
> because there was no room
> for them in the inn.
>
> Luke 2:7 (NIV)

SARAH'S GIFT

Outside, the first rays of daylight broke across the Judean hills. Already Sarah could hear the bleating of sheep, the banging and clanking of the village waking to another busy day. Never had there been so many strangers in Bethlehem! Never had they had so many guests!

Quickly Sarah ate the thick slice of buttered bread her mother gave her. "Sarah, we need—"

"Water," Sarah finished for mother. "We *always* need water!"

She picked up the big clay pot and headed down the dusty street toward the village well.

When Sarah returned home with the water, her father stood in front of the inn, waiting for her. "Was it busy at the well?" he asked, taking the big jar and heading toward the stable.

"It's busy everywhere, Papa!"

"That it is. I never thought I'd say business was *too* good, but I can't take in even one more guest—no matter who he is or what he's willing to pay!" He emptied the jar into a big trough. "Today we're going to need lots of—"

"Water!" Sarah said, taking the jar from his hand. "All I ever do is go for water! How boring!"

It was later that afternoon, as Sarah was coming back from another trip to the well, that she saw the couple. At first they looked just like any other travelers. They stopped in front of Sarah's door as the man helped the lady slide down from the donkey's back.

She's going to have a baby! Sarah thought, looking at the woman's wide, round belly. *And soon!*

The man knocked on the door of the inn. Papa stepped outside. He shook his head while he spoke. As Sarah came closer, she could hear his words. "No room, no room. We have no room here for you. I'm sorry."

"Please," the man said. "All the private homes are filled, too. Anything will do. My wife must have shelter and rest."

"No. I am sorry," Papa said firmly. "There is no more room!"

The couple stood near their donkey, talking quietly. "What shall we do, Joseph? It won't be long now. Must my baby be born in the street?"

"Mary," the man said gently, "our journey has been long, and you are tired. Let's get a fresh drink from the well. I'm sure God sees our problem and will not forget us."

"I have fresh water!" Sarah said, stepping closer. The lady looked up. How pale she was, and yet how beautiful!

"Thank you, little one," she said, lifting the water to her lips.

"You are most kind," the man said. "I am Joseph. This is my wife Mary. We have come to register for the tax."

"My father owns the inn," Sarah said, setting down the water pot.

"And the inn is full," Joseph sighed, turning the donkey to head back down the street. Just then, the door to the inn opened, and Sarah's father called to Joseph.

"The stable. You and your wife can stay in the stable."

Sarah was embarrassed. Perhaps they would think it insulting to be offered a place in a common stable. And Mary was so lovely....

Mary smiled at Sarah. "Let's see this stable of yours."

Sarah ran ahead, eager to make sure everything was ready. While Joseph tied their donkey nearby, Sarah helped Mary lie down on a soft mound of fresh straw.

"Thank you, little one," Mary said, closing her eyes.

"Sarah! Where are you, Sarah?" Mama called. "We need more water!"

"I have to go," she said, running toward the door, "but I'll be back!"

It was dark by the time Sarah finished her chores and started toward the stable. All was quiet, except for the sounds of animals chomping their fodder and the soft cooing of birds in the rafters overhead. "Mary," Sarah called.

Joseph stepped from behind the donkey stall. He put his finger to his lips. "Shh-shh. She is sleeping now."

"I brought you something to eat," Sarah said, showing him a napkin filled with cheese and figs.

Just then a frail sound filled the stable. Sarah's eyes widened. "Yes," Joseph smiled, "the baby has been born. Mary has a son!" He took Sarah's hand and led her to the far side of the stable, to a manger filled with straw. There, wrapped in strips of cloth, lay the newborn baby.

"He's beautiful!" Sarah whispered.

"His name is Jesus."

"Hello, Baby Jesus," Sarah said. She touched his tiny cheek with her finger, and his dark eyes turned toward her. Sarah felt a tingle inside as he stared up into her face. Such wonderful eyes!

Mary stirred on the pile of straw nearby. She looked very tired, but Sarah thought she was more beautiful than ever. "He is lovely, yes?" Mary asked.

"Oh, yes!" Sarah said. "I brought you some food."

Mary waved the napkin aside. "All I really need is...." She hesitated, looking up at Sarah.

"Water," Sarah smiled. "Want me to get you a fresh drink from the village well?"

Mary smiled. "That would be a wonderful thing, little one."

Sarah's sandals clattered on the cobblestone street. The clay jar felt cool in her arms. "A wonderful thing." The lovely lady had said those words. A fresh drink would be a *wonderful thing*. "Maybe fetching water isn't so boring after all," Sarah said aloud. And a bright star seemed to dance right over her stable.

A Closer Look

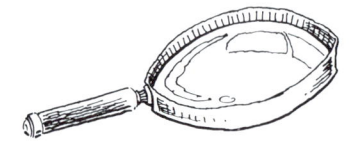

Do you sometimes feel that the things you have to do aren't really important? They may even seem *boring*—learning times tables and stacking dishes and folding clothes and delivering newspapers and watching your baby sister.

Because all of the family's water had to be drawn from the village well, Sarah spent a lot of her time filling and refilling the water jar. And sometimes she felt that was a really boring way to spend her day. But it's important to do your best in whatever you do, to offer the finest you have. For Sarah that was a clean stable and a cool drink of water.

What do you have to offer others? A kind word, a freshly baked cookie, a handmade card, a smile, a helping hand with Christmas packages. Give away something of yourself this very day!

What's Next?

Do you ever pretend you're one of the people in the Christmas story—a shepherd or a wise man or a woman who traveled beside Mary and Joseph on the way to Bethlehem? It's fun to imagine what you would have done, what you might have given to Baby Jesus. But it's not too late to offer the Christ child a gift. Can you guess what it could be? That's right! You can give Him your heart and your life. Would you like to do that right now? If so, pray this prayer:

>Dear Jesus, I'm bringing you a very special gift—
>me!
>I want to belong to You and be like You
>always!

☆ ☆ ☆

Fun Stuff

??Riddle??

I'm found in barns and filled with hay.
That is where the Christ child lay.
What am I?

To find the answer to this riddle, finish the puzzle below by writing the correct letter in the blank:

You find me in meat
   but not in beat. ____
I'm needed for seat
   but not for set. ____
You use me in been
   but not in bee. ____
I'm seen in gear
   but not in ear. ____
You'll spot me in bite
   but not in bit. ____
I appear in red
   but not in Ed. ____

The answer is: ____ ____ ____ ____ ____ ____

(See Answer Page.)

Wonderful Words

Have you ever noticed that the word *Christmas* is often written *Xmas*? This X is the Greek letter *chi*, the first letter of the Greek word for "Christ."

From Me to God

Thanks for Christmas. I know it's more than Santas and shopping and presents. I know, but sometimes I forget. So in the middle of buying and getting gifts, help me remember Your gift to us all—Baby Jesus.

Merry Christmas, God!

★　★　★

WEEK 13
Some New Year's Fun

God's Amazing Word

I [God] am making everything new!
Revelation 21:5 (NIV)

A HEAVY PROBLEM

Mary Beth reached into her Christmas stocking for another candy cane. "And you should have seen those desserts! Enough pies to feed four football teams. My grandma sure can bake!"

Ashleigh sat on the floor, looking at Mary Beth's Christmas presents. "What a great outfit!" she said, holding up a soft blue and white sweater and matching corduroy pants.

"Yeah…uh, I have to take it back."

"Why? Don't you like it?"

"Sure!" Mary Beth said, coming to sit beside Ashleigh. "But, well, it's too small."

"Oh," Ashleigh said, refolding the sweater. "Did you get any other clothes?"

Mary Beth looked down at her feet and sucked hard on her candy cane. When she finally looked up, there were tears in her eyes. "Yeah, I got some other clothes. And they were too small, too!"

"Oh," Ashleigh said. "Well, maybe the tags got messed up or something. Sometimes—"

"The tags aren't messed up," Mary Beth said, kicking the pile of new things. "*I'm* messed up!"

"What do you mean?"

"Look at me! I'm fat. Fat, fat, fat!"

"No, you're not... not really *fat*."

"Mama says I'm 'pleasingly plump' and Aunt Rachel says I'm 'chunky.' But they all mean *fat*." Mary Beth got up and pulled a tissue from the box on her dresser. "Do you have any idea what it's like to be the biggest one in your class? To dread the day the nurse takes your weight? To look like a beached whale every time you go swimming?"

"So, why don't you do something about it?" Ashleigh asked softly.

"Like what?" Mary Beth asked, rolling her tongue across the crook of the candy.

"Lose weight."

"I can't!" she said. "I've tried. Once I went a whole week without desserts and didn't lose even one crummy pound! I'm just a fatty forever. I can't change!"

"Of course you can change! My Uncle Gilbert quit smoking cigarettes last year—and he'd been smoking for twenty years!"

"Really?"

"Uh-huh. Then there's Aunt Rhinda. She decided to start walking every day—and lost twenty pounds!"

"Honest?"

Ashleigh nodded. "They both made New Year's resolutions."

"I've never made a New Year's resolution. Have you?"

Ashleigh stuck out her hands. "Last year I made a resolution not to bite my nails anymore." Mary Beth looked at the neat nails, painted a pale pink.

"What kind of resolutions could I make?" Mary Beth asked.

Ashleigh reached for a pad of paper lying on Mary Beth's

desk. In big letters she wrote: MY NEW YEAR'S RESOLUTIONS. "Well, something about your weight, right?" Mary Beth nodded. "How about 'I will exercise every day'?"

"Every day?"

"Sure. And how about desserts just once a week?"

"How about twice a week?" Mary Beth grinned.

"Okay. Twice a week. But no seconds at dinner. And no candy at lunch."

"What if I break my resolution?"

"Then you just begin again!" Ashleigh said. "Lots of times I'd be chewing on my nails without even realizing it. But I didn't give up because of that! I just kept trying until I could watch a whole TV show without once putting my hand near my mouth."

Mary Beth looked at the half-eaten candy cane in her hand. She looked at the pile of new clothes. "Let's put this list where I'll have to see it every day," she said, tossing the candy into the trash can. "And let's take the tags off that blue outfit. I'm going to keep it—and wear it before too long!"

"That wouldn't surprise me a bit!" Ashleigh laughed, taping the NEW YEAR'S RESOLUTIONS in the center of Mary Beth's mirror.

A Closer Look

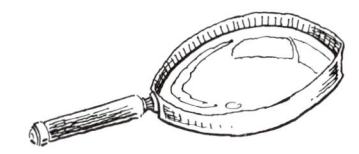

Is there something about yourself you don't like? That's only normal! But don't feel trapped by that trait or those habits. Remember Ashleigh's aunt and uncle? Even Ashleigh stopped biting her nails. People can change! But it takes hard work and determination and lots of "want-to." Did you know God longs for you to be the very best you can be? And He's waiting to help you do just that! Why not ask for His help right now?

What's Next?

Think of something you'd like to change about yourself. Maybe you'd like to be better at shooting baskets or playing the cello. Do you wish you could get better grades in school? How about keeping your room neat? Or reading your Bible every day? A resolution is really just a promise you make to yourself, a determination to do something. In the space below, make a NEW YEAR'S RESOLUTION, something that will *change* you for the better.

MY NEW YEAR'S RESOLUTION IS:

_____

Now, with God's help, work toward a new *you* in the new year!

☆   ☆   ☆

Fun Stuff

Look at the pictures on the next page. Underneath each one, write the first letter of that object. Then copy the letters into the blanks for a special holiday wish.

_ _ _ _ _

_ _ _ _   _ _ _ _ !

(See Answer Page.)

Tell Me Another One

Don't you love playing with new Christmas toys—bright red trucks and dress-up dolls and electronic games? Have you ever thought about someday designing toys for other boys and girls? Sometimes toys have very interesting beginnings....

John Spilsbury was a geography teacher in London, England, over two hundred years ago. He was always trying to find ways to help his students learn. One day he took a map of England and Wales, glued it to a piece of wood, and then cut it into pieces, using a saw with a very small blade. Next day he tried this *puzzle* with his students. They not only learned their geography lesson, they had fun doing it! Soon pictures as well as maps began appearing as puzzles. These puzzles are called jigsaw puzzles because of the special jigsaw blade still used for cutting them.

President Theodore Roosevelt was a famous outdoorsman. One day in 1902, while he was on a hunting expedition, President Roosevelt came upon a baby bear. He refused to shoot the cub. A businessman heard about the incident and decided to manufacture a toy cub. He called his creation "Teddy's bear." Today, *teddy bears* are the most popular stuffed animals in the United States.

Yo-yos were used by the early inhabitants of island jungles as weapons! The word comes from the Philippine language and means "to return."

From Me to God

Thanks for new years and fresh starts, God. With Your help, I'm going to be the best I can be, starting this very day!

★ ★ ★

Building a Better Me

How to Write a Christmas "Thank-You" Note

1. Try writing some thank-you notes. Hasn't Christmas been great? And wasn't it fun opening all those gifts? Now is the perfect time for you to say thanks for all your presents.

2. Begin with a clean sheet of paper. Lined stationery or notebook paper is best. The note doesn't have to be long or fancy. Just use your own words to show your appreciation for the present. Mention the gift and tell why you like it. The sample note below will help show you how:

Dear Grandma,

    Thanks for the sled. It's great! I will have lots of fun with it in the snow.

                             Love,
                             Brett

3. Put your thank-you in an envelope. Seal it and place a stamp on it. Make sure you *clearly* print or write the name and address of the person to whom it is going. Put your own return address in the upper lefthand corner.

Answer Page

Page 17 (See diagram.)

Page 24 (See diagram.)

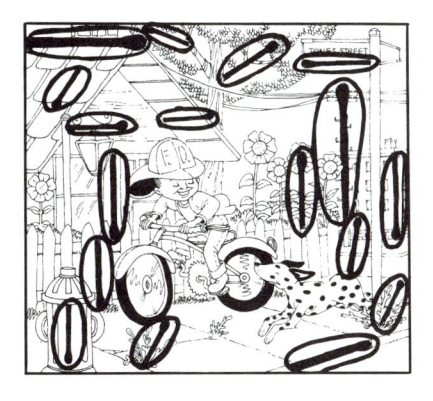

Page 32 (See diagram.)

Page 40   Success comes in can's, not in cannot's!

Page 49   (See diagram.)

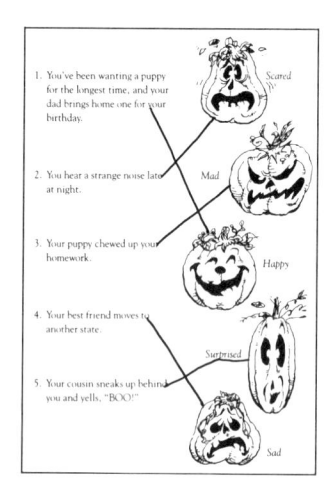

Page 51   There are 206 bones in the human body.

Page 61
1. cool
2. frost
3. rake
4. leaves
5. football
6. sweater
7. red
8. yellow
9. orange
10. pumpkin

Page 68   (See diagram.)

Page 78 and 79

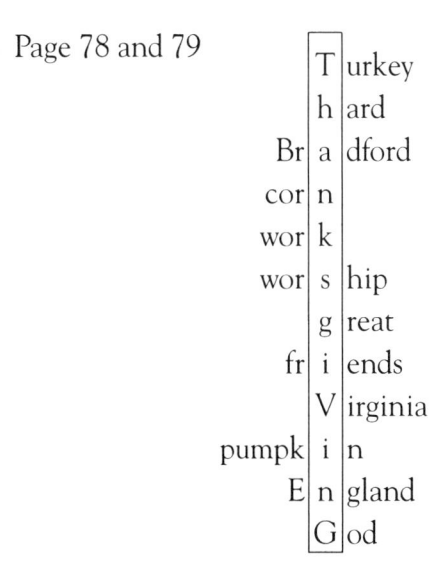

	T	urkey
	h	ard
Br	a	dford
cor	n	
wor	k	
wor	s	hip
	g	reat
fr	i	ends
	V	irginia
pumpk	i	n
E	n	gland
	G	od

Page 86 Reading is fun!

Page 97 Jesus is the reason for the season!

Page 114 Manger

Page 121 Happy New Year!

127